ONE THOUSAND YEARS

POEMS ABOUT THE HOLOCAUST

ONE THOUSAND YEARS

POEMS ABOUT THE HOLOCAUST

DAVID RAY

Timberline Press
Fulton, Missouri
2004

ACKNOWLEDGEMENTS:
Some of the poems in *One Thousand Years* (a few of them in variant versions) have appeared in the following publications:

"A Day at a Time" in *The Iowa Review*; "Half a Skull" in *Kansas Quarterly* and *Demons in the Diner*; "Mingo, Oklahoma" in *The Chariton Review*; "World War II" in *New Letters* and *Wool Highways*; "Come and See" in *Prairie Schooner*; "A Couple of Survivors" in *AWP Newsletter* and *Blood to Remember: American Poets on the Holocaust*; "The Musician" in *GSU Review* (received Honorable Mention in the Miriam Lindberg Israel Poetry Peace Prize 2002, Tel Aviv, Israel), "For Rudolf Hoess, Commandant of Auschwitz" in *Prairie Schooner* and *Demons in the Diner*; "Fascism Again" in *TIWA*; "The Man Who Can Remember Only One Minute" in *Crazyhorse*; "Good News at the Alpine Villa" in *Kansas Quarterly*; "Sightseeing in the Reich" in *New Letters*; "One Thousand Years" in *Paterson Literary Review*; "Bronja's Deli" (as "In the Delicatessen") in *Ironwood*; "Upstate" in *Prairie Schooner*; "Geisteskrankheit" in *West Branch*; "Grace Under Fire" was a finalist in the 2003 Strokestown Poetry Contest, Ireland; "The Way with Dissent" in *Dragging the Main*; "The Weeping" in *Potpourri*; "Talking to Sheep in New Zealand" (as "Scientific Management") in *Wool Highways*.

Text copyright © 2004 by David Ray
Cover artwork © by David Levinthal: *Untitled* from series *Mein Kampf, 1993-94*. Polaroid Polacolor ER Land Film, 20x24 inches.
Design by Judy Ray

ISBN 0-944048-30-7

Timberline Press
6281 Red Bud, Fulton, Missouri 65251

for those who survived and those who did not

CONTENTS

"Good Lord, what is man! for as simple he looks,
Do but try to develop his hooks and his crooks,
With his depths and his shallows, his good and his evil..."
Robert Burns

"You believe in a palace of crystal that can never be destroyed—
a palace at which one will not be able to put out one's tongue or
make a long nose on the sly. And perhaps that is just why I am
afraid of this edifice, that it is of crystal and can never be
destroyed and that one cannot put one's tongue out at it even on
the sly...But while I am alive and have desires I would rather my
hand were withered off than bring one brick to such a building."
—Dostoyevsky, *Notes from Underground*

A DAY AT A TIME

for Victor Klemperer

"Anyone who does not lose his reason over certain things
has no reason."
  – Gottfried Lessing

Just walking down the street
you have to heil Hitler many times.
You go shopping for meat
but the sign is in the window
and the butcher waves you away.

Don Carlos is banned because
on stage he said something
favoring the theme of freedom,
and an actor is shot for telling
a joke about Hitler. Another tax

is levied, but only against Jews,
another oath of loyalty required,
this time *eternal*, requiring a triple
Sieg Heil. *A Farewell to Arms*
is banned, too pacifist, soon all

books by non-Aryans are pulled
from the shelves. You find that
you're banned from the reading
room. They take back your card.
At home you read quickly, knowing

that soon your books will be burned.
Two policemen drop by to pick up
your ration card—no more cigarettes
or chocolate or gas for the jalopy
you love. At the American Embassy

you are told that your number is
56,429 and your wife's is 56,430,
but it is not likely any visas will be
approved although back in America
the policies are being reviewed.

Patience is advised. The two policemen
return to search the house for weapons.
You tell them you have an old saber
from when you served the fatherland
in the Great War, but you don't know

where it is, that saber. They insist
on helping you find it—the task
takes a few hours, everything
turned upside down, inside out.
Basement and attic are ransacked.

At last the saber turns up in a trunk.
You go along to the station to be
charged for the crime, harboring
a weapon. Soon they come back
to collect your typewriter. It must be

tiresome for the policemen, you say
to your wife, to come back so often,
one time for this, the next for that—
the family silver, the radio—and to make
the Inventory of Assets, possessions

they will steal as soon as they kill you.
There is always something overlooked,
or which some bureaucrat has now
thought of. Your professorship, of course,
was the first thing to go, your pension

cut down almost to nothing. You keep
hoping a job will turn up in Japan or India
or South America. A friend writes how
it's green there—you know what she means.
You ask yourself if you're going to hang on

until it is too late—for months friends
have been saying goodbye—they got out.
You ask yourself this every day, long after
it's too late. The language they use is not
the German you learned as a child.

When the Führer says he will *swear in blood,*
he means murder. You can't take your mother
to the hospital lest she be euthanized.
You are told your house must be sold but
that you will be given seven and a half percent.

You notice how, as long as there is alcohol
and gasoline, drunk driving seems an attractive,
often fatal, diversion. You note that "veronal
in a hotel room" is sometimes the answer.
You see that many, e.g., yourself, are blacking out,

going blind for minutes, even hours, at a time.
You observe that there are potholes and mud craters
on all roads but the magnificent, much-glorified
Autobahn, shown off to foreigners. You perceive
that meadows and woods, lovely as ever, wait

it out for the hell to be over. You agree that once
the Olympics are over it will be open season
on those without sabers, typewriters, telephones,
jobs, radios, silver, pensions, houses, cars, books,
synagogues, rifles, machine guns, tanks, cavalry,

bombers, fighter planes, grenades, trenchcoats,
motorcycles, swastika armbands, maps, garroting
ropes, poison pellets, firing squads, friends
from abroad, homelands (fatherlands, motherlands),
visas, passports, adequate disguises, escape routes.

A NAZI POET

> "And nought of *Rome* in *Rome* perceiv'st at all."
> — Edmund Spenser

When Albert Speer designed a new Berlin
for Hitler's Third Reich—a city of marble,
with little subtlety and hardly a tree
in sight, with the people to be added later—

he planned building in an assured self-
destruction, making sure each edifice
would fall into ruins on schedule, looking
Roman, nothing like the bombed-out city.

The cracks and weaknesses and stresses
would all be in the right places to crumble
in a classical sequence, symphonic,
to the accompaniment of Wagnerian

music. Though Speer may have known
that his toy buildings were also an apt
metaphor, I doubt if he told his Führer,
who often delighted to play with the models.

THE PERIMETERS OF GRIEF

He had in mind a one thousand year Reich,
and one thousand years it shall be,
for the grief must be included, the thousand
year Kaddish. It will take one thousand years
for the monsters to finish their death throes,
at last purged of the poison they spewed.

It will take one thousand years for the last print
of *Triumph of The Will* to crumble to dust,
for those flickering shadows to fall the rest
of the way into darkness, for those torch-lit
faces, thousands caught in hypnotic trance,
to leave off their worshipful gaze at the sky,

awaiting Herr Hitler, their Savior, descending
out of the clouds, touching ground as if
he were Christ in his robes, blessing his people.
Did they think he could raise even their own
dead when the battles were over? It will take
one thousand years for the last lie of Goebbels

to be swept into the tomb and for the guilty
to admit guilt and hand back a fraction of the loot.
It will take a thousand years for blood to be worn
away from the charnel house, for the bell tolling
to reach the last name in the *Totenbuch*—one thousand
years too late for the human to be touched with humanity.

EMILY'S DIARY

for Emily Carr

Of each year, at its outset, she wrote
"It will be a good year." 1934,
a good one. 1939, a good one,
"full of peace," she predicted,
"and much joy in nature and from
all things around us." She drove
her covered wagon into the forest.

While they were killing
she was painting, on old driftwood
half the time. While they
were stacking their dead
she was having a cup, sharing
her crumbs with a file of ants,
steady, devoted, as if taking orders.

And when they were making peace
yet again, because they could never
quite win, she was writing again
in her diary. "A good year,"
she blessed the new one, and hugged
a young tree "before it got too fat."
Then she whispered in the ear
of her pony, nibbled a few of his oats.

And drew her shawl tight,
for she knew her hopes were just hopes
and no more and the forests were blazing.

A SONG FOR HERR HITLER

Where did he kiss them, darling children,
as he held them on his knee, Adolf Hitler—

making his rounds, campaigning,
with a stop here and there while his aides

passed out ice cream and flowers,
flags to wave and bright arm-bands?

He did not say "Suffer the little children
to come unto me," but it was something

like that, as he patted and kissed them
like an uncle or affectionate father

or like Jesus. On the forehead, that's where
he kissed them, the children of Germany,

on their soft Aryan brows, and his fatherly palm
drew them close. And where, you might ask,

did he pat and caress them, the little children
who climbed on his knees or were placed there?

On their shoulders and rumps, on their knees
and their thighs—that's where he patted

and stroked them and caressed them,
on their hair most of all—the little children

of Germany, who were almost all perfect.
And what did he say to them, this master

of words, this leader so loved that he
could do as he wished with the children,

pat them or poke them or send them on
some distant journey? What did he say

when he pinched their soft rosy cheeks
and their thighs? Not so much, really,

just short words of affection, like the ones
his dogs understood as he patted and petted them

as he did the children of Germany while he gazed
into their eyes, which gazed back, dazed,

often blue, sometimes brown or green
or hazel or sprinkled with stars. And where

you might well ask, did he send them,
the children, who were so plentiful and perfect?

Where did he, Der Führer, father of his Third
Reich, where in the world did he send them?

To Poland and Russia, that's where he sent them,
and to Denmark and France and to fly over England,

to fall in fuel fire, to spin onto the sea, that's where
he sent them. And to other lands too, for his hands

patted children but also reached far across oceans
and deserts and seas. And where did he scatter them,

the children, where did he, Adolf Hitler, scatter them?
On the snow, in the air, in the sea's darkest depths,

19

on the steppes and the mountains, in the fire,
in the mud and runoff from clay, in the rain

and hot sand, in the clouds and grey fogs,
on green trees and soft furs of four-legged creatures,

on feathers of birds and roofs of old tombs—
that's where he scattered them, and elsewhere as well.

And his fatherly hand may reach out through the years
seeking his children of ash and charred bone, lest

they be left alone with no father like him, rare indeed,
and unique, one of a kind. Or so you might hope.

HALF A SKULL

A skull in my hands—
could well be the earth, zigzag
roads etched deep, woe map—

least valued of bones,
a clay bowl fashioned by hand,
yellowed welkin flipped

like a turtle's back
with a thumbflick. Yet evil
starts here, burns, broods thick

as smog. Cain had one,
Abel too. Mountains of these
appear here and there

not much mourned, soon greened
over or dust-heaped, not worth
much, least important

yet also the most—
dome of my joy, roofed haven
for bliss, sole retreat

safe from those masters
who would even now delight
to order this slave

whipped bloody-backed, fling
salt on the wounds. Wind would clean
mine too, where I touch.

BERUF

Beruf = Duty, Calling, Profession

Himmler stood by a mass grave,
got splattered with brains as his men
shot into the bodies below, piling up
in layer after layer, blood flowing
freely as water. Was there even
a moment's remorse?

No, although he did regret
seeing such a sight, soiling
his hands. Having *ordered*
should have been enough
of a *Beruf.* Pontius Pilate
did not watch crucifixions.

There is never a shortage
of war criminals. Pol Pot
killed millions. Their faces
still stare out of portraits,
snapped as they were led
to the next room, an abattoir.
On a rainy day I wander in
to an exhibit where they
have been mounted on walls,
                    treated as art.

Our own victims remain faceless,
incinerated, blown off the earth
from miles high, by airmen
who do not have to face them—
not as the S.S. with his machinegun,
not as the Khmer Rouge
or Death Squads trained

22

at the School of the Americas.
We have not had to deal with bodies
for years. We have been spared
the obscenities. We have not
had to wash brains off our glasses.

THE BLACK FOREST

She remembers the forest,
     the famous Black Forest,
         she and her brother
cowering there,
     hidden in shadows
         like Hansel and Gretel,
smuggled out
     over the mountains
         across the river,
sleeping in log huts.
     She remembers this
         and most of all
the fat woman who hugged
     the two children lifting
         them up into her arms
though she was German,
     this woman, and her man
         gone with his axe
into Poland, burning
     the fields, throwing flames
         into the homes,
hanging men on their own gate-
     posts, on schoolyard
         swings, prodding
children with guns, children
     with their arms raised
         as if making an H
or about to fall in prayer.
     She recalls all this
         and the names of those
who did not emerge
     from the forest,
         the Black Forest,

who were not hugged,
      lifted up by the kindly
            woman, the German.

INNOCENCE

Don't blame the bricks
though they're blood red.

Not one volunteered
to serve, be a wall.

JANINA

for Janina David

She didn't know how
        to cross herself right,
                but she tried, little Janina,

saved from the fate
        of others in Warsaw—
                all her others—mother,

father, aunts, uncles,
        grandparents. In the convent
                she pretended to love

black bread, mumbled the prayers,
        and raved against Jews
                when she had to

in order to remain invisible—
        whatever it took—
                and thus Janina survived.

MINGO, OKLAHOMA

Mulberries stained the rotten steps
of the church like drops of purple rain.
Sis and I sat in the branches
and though her mouth was stained
I sat too proud to eat such fare.

I sulked. I brooded. Across the road
children with parents played games
that excluded us. They never stopped
hating us, and enjoyed their breakfast
more because we two were locked out.

Sometimes we made a nest for ourselves
in the weeds, walled them out,
but now we had climbed into the tree.
One way or the other, I vowed,
I would save the life of my sister.

And thus I leapt down and ran
from door to door yelling until
they came for us and took us off to jail
in the orphanage. In a distant land
Dr. Mengele was cutting girls in half, twins.

I did not know of such things, not yet.
I knew only that Sister and I were hungry,
hurting, and that there were people
who would cut us up if they could.

WORLD WAR II

Boys all over the world
burned trash in cardboard boxes,
imagined Hitler dying in flames.
It took years for the grownups
      to make that happen.

Hitler crouched back
in red curling corners,
and when his walls crumbled
we stomped him, at least
in Oklahoma, where at night
we crouched in fear
of his bombers. Fear
brought everything close,
      Japan, Germany.

At home my stepfather's hands
roamed over the thighs
of my sister. I turned
the pages of *Life*, sought
my father in photographs
of men wading swamps,
their rifles held high over
their heads. I feared
the Japs would get him
for sure before he could get
back to save us—me
and that whimpering girl.

There were many theatres of war.

THE UNCERTAINTY PRINCIPLE

"Count no man fortunate
who is not dead. Only
the dead are free of pain."
                    – Sophocles

Even as we danced to the jukebox
I Don't Want to Set the World on Fire

they were doing just that all over Europe.
Though born too young or already too old

for this war or that, are we still fodder,
untested as both victims and perpetrators,

putty that brainwash may yet seduce
and deform though the face may declare

the innocence of infancy intact to the end?
Count no man free of evil until his death,

for only the dead have the right to boast.
Quod erat Demonstrandum: to be human

is to be a part of it, all of it.

SPAIN

I spoke today of the Spanish Civil War, which none
of them had heard of, being born far too late
and too indifferent. I spoke of Francisco Franco
and King Alfonso and Lorca who was shot
and Guernica the bombed fishing village, the dive
bombers, screaming Stukas, and the hands flung up
to the skies. I spoke of the red Spanish earth
used as a testing ground for the big war ahead,
a murderous warm up while the Allies did nothing.
I spoke of the Hegelian dialectic crunching its way
like an old ratchet serving a rusty well in the rocky
ground, and I described the Spanish village
where I lived for a winter, where some of the men
had not emerged from hiding places in attics
and cellars thirty years after the war. Franco
was still alive and much feared. I recalled for them
the churchyard on the hill with its pockmarked walls
where firing squads had helped neighbors settle disputes.
And last I spoke of how as a boy in Oklahoma I saw
the skinny man with an eye patch and a crutch instead
of the leg he had left in Spain when he fought
in the Lincoln Brigade. Almost in tears I told how
we boys taunted him and made fun of his black beret
as he sat on the curb outside the Oasis Bar and Grill.
I mentioned how he was condemned by every drunk
inside the tavern as a Commie. And then I spoke
of how I wish I had gone and sat beside him.

ECHOLALIA

Europe bleeds again.
I am old enough to know
it promised not to.

"COME AND SEE"

The Nazi officer in a long leather coat shoves his Luger
against the head of a Russian boy and with his left hand
like a bear's claw on the skull forces him to his knees

while three others stand by, their uniforms impressive.
One holds a can of gasoline. Another has a flamethrower
strapped on his back and the third, goggles still on

since he's just climbed off his motorcycle, holds a long
dagger handy. It's a scene so horrific that I find myself praying
it's fake, no more than an old movie still, although

it is bad enough that the scene may be based on something
that once was real. I crave reassurance, thus study with care
to make sure. And I am relieved to learn that the picture

is fake, the Nazis in costume just actors, the grimacing boy
a child movie star. A sneer on the officer's face gives away
his inept pretending. We know how they do it in real life,

hardly glancing at victims, kicking bodies to make sure
they are dead, not wanting to waste bullets. Cinema Nazis
throw shadows too stark for this landscape, and it's hard

to fake the callous insouciance of killers. The boy's an old
man in Russia. Elsewhere the grandsons of survivors
blast away as their leader claims to have a plan he'll share later.

PANTOPHOBIA

Christians may watch for four horsemen
who never arrived for two millennia,
but those horsemen are far down
on my list. At its head are missiles
still in the ground, the ones we're still
on target for and others with which
we may destroy nations. I work down
through asteroids—future, not past.
Global warming is also fearful
although our leaders don't think so.

I have conquered my fear of sharks
and my terror of elevators is only
a flashback to childhood, no more
vivid than what's in the air, worse
every day. With such a list—since
a pantophobic fears everything—
it is wise to work at transcendence.

Yet I have not run off to an ashram
or cave to chant prayers day and night.
Crusades, Inquisition, and Holocaust
gallop into my dreams as I fear the fourth.

A COUPLE OF SURVIVORS

He was a G.I. and she was huddled with the others,
abandoned in a booby-trapped bicycle factory
when the noises closed in and the shouts were not
German and the tin door slid open—a man framed
in grey light. She was sixteen and the first to face him—
a man with his rifle, an American captain, struck dumb,
cagey, still looking around for the guards who had fled
into the forest, but not before setting the explosives.
Only a heavy rain had prevented their going off.

She said in German "I am a Jew" and he said
"I am too," and stepped back, asking her to show him
the others. And then, as she tells it decades later,
with that one gesture of respect he restored her to humanity.
Then together they led the other women out into the rain.
He too, husband to her, remembers blasting open
the tin door, sliding it back, beholding her for the first
time—his sixteen-year-old sixty eight pound future wife.
It is such a sacred memory, the first smile on her stunned face.

1936 OLYMPICS, BERLIN

The only way they could explain
was that Jesse Owens
must have Aryan blood.

How did it get there,
flowing inside a black man,
and how had he managed

to obscure it, perhaps with a drug?
But the doctors could not
work fast enough to enable

a reversal, claim him as Aryan.
It had already been observed
in the showers that his color

was not just makeup or paint.
If only the fraud could be
exposed...*if only*... the Führer

might yet find a use for him.
Meanwhile, best to let all
Aryans boo and jeer him,

look for those who took part
in this fraud. Even so
is empowered the indignant

rage of the Reich seeking Justice!

FOR RUDOLF HOESS,
COMMANDANT OF AUSCHWITZ

"Did they serve life? Or injure it?"
— Vikram Seth, *The Golden Gate*

Rudolf, I used to teach your prose
as proof that words are often used more
to hide than convey what a writer means.
You recalled yourself as a boy and how
you threw yourself down in the snow,
arms out. Angels appeared. Later you stood
like Nebuchadnezzar watching the furnace,
and it made you sad, tired too as more
than one Daniel, more than one Anne,
writhed into ash. It was hard work,
you pointed out again and again. No one
knew how you suffered from the strain
of your calling—your sacred *Beruf*, rigid
as John Calvin's. I contrasted your self-
satisfied memoirs with Anne Frank's, used
an excerpt in which she feared she might do
the least creature harm. With names removed
from these paragraphs I invited my students
to guess who had written your words,
who hers. You came out the winner, she
the failure, at life. As "an industrialist, a very
practical man, maybe wealthy—definitely
successful, a workaholic," you were an
admirable guy. The anonymous Anne
was much older "an anxious type, a male,
or perhaps a battered wife who did not
understand her feelings, most likely needed
a psychiatrist." Both of you, it seemed,
"were deeply religious." How easy it is
to lie, I thought, easy when making speeches,

easy when writing diaries or memoirs!
Books with pages once unsullied as snow
emerged from your years—Anne's *Diary*,
your *Totenbuchen*, ledgers crammed with names
in elegant script, those who went to the showers,
the ovens. As an industrialist you were so efficient
you could have told what each brought to the flames
or the warehouses and where they had lived,
been plucked from their beds. Your records
kept account of their hair and their gold,
jewels and clothing abandoned, suitcases
to be used again back in the fatherland. Half
a world away, decades later, we debate evil,
try to fix the moment a man becomes pure
with it, good wholly burned out of his skull.
Yet as you awaited your trial you insisted
your motives were mixed. You had to please
someone. Was it God? Your father? Wife who
waited with dinner? Surely it was not the children
you took on your lap. Perhaps it was that man
in Berlin who had captured your faith. Goebbels
called Hitler adorable, killed his daughters lest
they live on without such a godfather. Somewhere,
Rudolf, we have to draw the line, firm and clear—
even as a Nazi scribe would. A man can tiptoe up
to that line, yet he must not cross it. Still, you argued
your innocence, insisted you were only following
orders as a dutiful officer must. Have we not heard
that phrase often? Nobody's perfect, but Rudolf,
I think you had crossed the line—the kind we must
fear in ourselves. We back away from judgement
of those who are like you, yet our own. They too
are good providers, good family men. They have
their reasons—impeccable economics. Arms sales
keep the great game afloat. When you threw yourself

down in the snow, made an angel, you had not yet
followed the wolf's call. But why wrong the wolf?
In molten Rudolf only the saint would discern
flecks of base goodness, still holding out. Your
achievement was almost pure and perfect—evil
to the last tenth of a tenth—though once a boy
threw himself down in the snow, made an angel.
Ash of your years, Hoess, afflicts heaven still.

UNDSOWEITER

As if God can bless
only one at a time,
the top dog triumphs.

And yet the devil
seems more resourceful,
allows an orgy of evil.

FASCISM AGAIN

The kid who shoots down an airliner
      and laughs at it
            is somebody's cousin.

Those men accepting roses and kisses
      are just back
            from the killing fields.

The child lifted in arms
      will be happy and evil,
            much-mourned after his war.

The ghosts of Berliners still play
      violins on the snowbanks
            of Stalingrad.

Puffballs of poison
      drift over the cities.
            None are spared.

In the Pacific junk of old wars
      is tipped off barges—
            "Out of sight out of mind!"

Bald battlefields rejoice
      and grow hair again.
            Women who made

weapons on assembly lines
      weep for their grandsons.
            Napoleon's knee

is still twitching. Hitler rides
            a trike in the suburbs.
                        Letters from fathers

rot in ancient mailbags.
            The latest morale study
                        shows pressing need

for war. Nothing else quite works out.
            Women comb hair
                        till they bleed. Each

might have stopped one
            of the warriors, hurled
                        her son from the wall.

ANIMAL INTELLIGENCE

On the terrace at dusk
we take up our discourse
on animals, some insisting
they are dumb, then me
telling how the octopus

learns with only one lesson
to open the jar, unscrewing
the lid, tentacles flung
around the glass, clutching
it,then reaching in for the prize.

It's hard to think of that trick
as dumb. And another octopus
learns it from watching it done
just once, whereas I have tried
for a year to learn Tai Chi,

but still stumble. I mention
the hammer-shaped stones
that lobsters have been seen
to clutch in their claws
at the bottom of the ocean.

"And plants too, of course,"
I add, "all quite intelligent."
I am met with derision, dared
to prove it. "Only this morning,"
I say, "up high on a cactus,

a blossom aimed right
at the sun, looking right at it,
knowing just where to look.
Everywhere there is this
wondrous intelligence."

Except us, I did not say.

HORSES

Swift knew that horses are far more noble
than people. Raskolnikov pondered his own

crime when he saw a man beating a horse.
George Orwell saw a horse being whipped

by a boy in an English village, was inspired
to write *Animal Farm,* in which people are pigs.

Monty the horse whisperer speaks into the ear,
uses the art of seduction. My father broke

horses and sons the old fashioned way, by beating.
In New York a man is tried for assaulting a horse,

hitting hard with his fists. But no one has brought
to justice those who forced horses into the paths

of artillery, machine guns, the sword, the pike
and the tank, and made them herd people like cattle.

Man can be ingenious when he designs to save lives
or to kill. What could be more clever than the mother

bomb designed to give birth in mid-air, or the medieval
"man-catcher"—long pole with a spring trap to thrust

around a man's neck so that he can be pulled down,
that his head may be sliced off with a sword?

But the crime of all time is to drag a horse
                              down to the level of man.

GEBURTSTAG

> "The pomp and grandeur of evil
> Soon passes, but always a new
> Pustule opens somewhere on the earth."
> — Kenneth Rexroth, *The Dragon and the Unicorn*

In Deutschland they are celebrating his birthday
and a spokesman describes him as a second Napoleon,

adding that the Holocaust ovens were built by the allies
after the war, nothing but propaganda. Thucydides

gave us little chance of waking from history's nightmare
and not repeating our mistakes every twenty years.

In Berlin they'll have a parade and *Deutschland
Uber Alles* is to be played by a brass band,

and souvenir mugs bearing the Führer's face
are quite popular. In Utah and Idaho blond children

with blue eyes are taught the scripture of hate.
Popular in several American cities are shooting

ranges where you can rent weapons of World War II
as well as those of the Korean, Vietnam, and Iraq.

Old vets say there's nothing like cradling again
in arms the machine gun of your choice.

SURVIVORS

When the instructor turned on the slide
projector and a wall in the dark room
exploded into color—Picasso's painting
of the bombing of Guernica—a girl
from Spain began screaming and threw
her arms up like a woman in the painting.
Then she crawled under a table.

Years later an elderly dinner guest
on her way out of our living room
stood stunned when she noticed
a framed photograph on our wall.

A horseman on a snow-covered slope
sat watching a herd of cattle
winding for miles, a long snaking queue.
I myself had sometimes seen in the picture
a blur of soldiers—maybe Napoleon's,
maybe Hitler's, retreating from Moscow.

But this woman went pale as the snow
until I assured her that the scene
was a cowboy in charge of a roundup
in Montana, 1943. The horseman
was not a guard, but only a cowboy,
and the photograph had been printed in *Life*,
              which was only a magazine.

SPLITTING HAIRS

"He had not experienced the most extreme of situations."
— Survivor quoted by biographer Nina Sutton

Bruno Bettelheim and others were blamed and scorned
even by certain survivors because they did not suffer

enough or were not interred in the worst of the death camps,
had survived the comforts of Dachau instead of Auschwitz,

as if on the scale of suffering the professor was too low
on the ladder. His abuse was premature, over and done with

by the time so many were herded into gas chambers. Some
were enraged that my professor had survived at all to teach us

and to heal psychotic children, putting to work his insights
into the sickest and most infantile minds of all—the killers

and arsonists and throwers of temper tantrums who made
all Europe their playpen, though for those unfortunate years

meant to be the first of one thousand years of Third Reich
they lacked a therapist with the skills of Dr. Bruno Bettelheim.

"THE OLDEST STORY EVER TOLD"

After Romain Gary

A survivor named Schoenbaum fled Germany
as soon as he could get a visa, and found himself
in La Paz in the high Sierras of Bolivia.
He opened a tailor shop and got to work,
and one day he discovered another survivor—
also a tailor from Poland—but this man,
Gluckman, insisted that he was named Pedro
and was only a humble driver of llamas.

He denied everything about his past
and seemed to be living in a ghost town
rather than La Paz. At times he would break out
with the Kaddish, as if lamenting the lost millions.
Schoenbaum saw that Gluckman was terrified,
so fearful of the Nazis that he could not believe
there was now a nation called Israel and that he
would be welcome there. Gluckman, a.k.a. Pedro,
could not believe that Germany was a nice
democratic country or that Hitler was long dead.

Gluckman suspected a plot to lure all Jews to Israel
for a new Holocaust, to finish off his people.
He knew for sure it would happen all over again,
and Schoenbaum could not convince him otherwise.
One night in the week of Yom Kippur
Schoenbaum followed Gluckman to find out
why he sneaked out each night with a basket
of food under his arm, disappearing into another
neighborhood. Who could be worthy of such charity?

At last Schoenbaum caught up, and peered down
through a skylight into a room where a man sat

at a table lit by a kerosene lamp. Like a waiter
Gluckman was serving this man, laying out sausage,
a bottle of beer, bread, red pimentos, a napkin.
The diner grunted something in German, and Gluckman
apologized, reached back into the basket for a cigar
he had forgotten, then lit it. As the match flared
Schoenbaum saw that Gluckman was smiling
with fixed, burning eyes, almost maniacal. At last
the man being served turned his head and Schoenbaum
saw a face he could never forget—it was Schultze,
the S.S. Commandant of the Torenberg death camp.

Schultze had made Gluckman his favorite victim,
torturing him daily for over a year. Schoenbaum,
almost in shock, wondered how such a scene
was possible. Am I dreaming? he wondered.
He waited, then followed Gluckman down an alley
and confronted him in the moonlight. "How can you?"
he demanded of Gluckman, who answered with a voice
that sounded as if it came out of the dark ages of history.
"Because…" he stuttered, "Schultze has promised
                    to treat me better next time."

ALZHEIMER'S AND OTHER BLESSINGS

Bless the man who can only remember
one minute, for he is free of history.

THE MAN WHO CAN REMEMBER
ONLY ONE MINUTE

> "Everything is fresh and new to him, embarrassingly so."
> – Neurologist

Each time you come into my room
I leap up rejoicing.
It's the first time I've ever seen you
and I've just been awake for a moment.
It is joy, reunion, celebration.
I take you in my arms and you smile
but say you are getting a bit tired of it
since I've done this a hundred
times already today, maybe a thousand.
Yet you are not altogether displeased,
pointing out how I failed to recall
the long hours gone past in which
I have jotted down—or at least you say so—
4:43 and I've just woken up,
the world is aglow.
4:44 and the sun is shining
and when I tell you I don't know how
or why those statements are there
you ask if it isn't my handwriting.
How the hell do I know, I shout,
yes, it looks like my writing
but I didn't write it. You sit me down
at a piano and I sing along. My fingers
do it all by themselves. No, I don't
know why, how, nor why it's a drop
off a cliff when I stop, begin shaking.
Grief's dead, I know that, a numbness
I'm glad for. And so much you say
you'd like to forget too. I hold you,
poor thing with that ragbag

of picnics remembered, of days
gone stale as bread. I am free of them.
I kiss you. Oh, how wonderful,
I cry out, you are here. I kiss you
for the first time. Your sore cheeks,
you say, pushing me back. A thousand
kisses today, you say, no more please.
But this is the first, a marvel.
We are here, in the moment.
You say it's what philosophers
pray for, and I've got for nothing.
Poor dear, I cannot even guess
how it must be to remember.
Try me tomorrow. Come to me then.
How marvelous! You are here.
I have just woken up, one minute
past. a.m. or p.m.? How the hell
should I know? I wish you'd not ask.
You have brought me this wonderful
brew, this magical taste. Coffee, you say,
yet it is new to me. I've never had it before.
And you've not been out to the village.
You say it's my fault, and is this how
I like it? How would I know, I keep asking.
Oh, gorgeous, and you in my arms,
that softness on my face. Never before.
You say often, all morning. It's the first time.
Oh, darling, I hope there will be yet another.
And this cup, so empty, what is it doing
beside us? Perhaps you can fill it, bring
something. Coffee, you say.
I will try it.

AT PLAY IN THE LABYRINTH

AVIS
LES JEUX
SONT
INTERDITS
DANS LE
LABYRINTHE
– Sign at the Jardin des Plantes, Paris

Walt Bodine, as Kansas City talk show host,
could hold forth on any subject,
chat up any guest, including the survivor
who had been found among corpses
at Auschwitz and nursed back to life
with an eye dropper. "And what about
laughter?" Walt asked. "Was there ever
occasion for laughter or humor at Auschwitz?"

"Oh, yes," she answered, "we would talk
about food day and night, laughing at how
we'd eat everything in sight after the war
and have a big party when Hitler died.
But the funniest thing of all was the time
we girls took off our clothes and had
a beauty contest. Whoever had the prettiest
boobs would get a piece of bread for a prize.
And can you guess who won?"

Walt, struck speechless, allowed a rare long
silence to intervene before his guest provided
the answer. "I did." She giggled like a school
girl, one of the naked, silly girls in a barracks
at Auschwitz. Walt cleared his throat.
"Congratulations," he said, and got back
to the grim humorless archeology
                                          . of death camps.

PAINTING PONTITO

When I recreate the town, as real
as I can make it, I sometimes improve it,

do away with half—as there's no need
for downspouts and gutters or a tangle

of wires overhead. When we *ragazzi*
ran through the streets, wore down

stones with our shoes or bare feet,
we often ducked out of sight, avoiding

snipers, priests, soldiers, old men back
from America. With paint I've wiped

them all out, since most were unkind.
I hear there's a weapon like that now,

not just my artistry—a bomb that kills
with neutrons, harms nothing I might

wish to bring back to life. Pale days
of our lives need not be revived

from oblivion. In fact, empty streets
are best. Who would prefer

the hard men of Rome to my stones?
I've left all the blood off, saving the red

for roof tile. What I'm trying to say
is that if I render my town virginal,

before its corruption, fresh as dawn,
every portal washed clean, I can survive

without faces. I need only stones, fresh dew
on the grass, not one face, *grazie mille*.

GOOD NEWS AT THE ALPINE VILLA

They did not damage anything, at least not much,
our hostess remarked of the wartime Nazis,
billeted there at the villa. Hobnail boots, she said,
had not dug deep or scarred the floors. They were
gentlemen, elite officers from Silesia and Berlin,
not so harsh and bad-mannered as foes from other
areas more populated by peasants, farmers, tradesmen.
Of course there were no Jews in Lombardy. In groups
of two or three, always well-dressed, the gentlemen
of the S.S. were charming when shopping in the village.
They learned some Italian, paid for their purchases.
They loved Pinocchio dolls carved by local craftsmen
and bought cameos to send home to their Frauleins.
In this villa furniture did not become firewood, she noted,
showing us museum quality antiques such as her bed.
Of all the Old Masters only a small Cranach disappeared
when they left—she's not saying they were perfect,
but they were decent chaps. Most likely the partisans,
rude peasants all, made off with the painting. The Germans
left untouched almost everything—green trees, snow,
the sapphire blue lake in which they dumped gold bars
still sought by divers, spoils of war. And oh, yes, they signed
the guest book upon departure, which shows they had nothing
to be ashamed of. You can look, she said, adding that not
one partisan signed, as most were illiterate. It still distressed
her that they dealt so rudely with Mussolini. The charm
of her elite S.S. guests was much missed, she said, putting us
on our best behavior lest we not measure up. She toasted us
farewell with wine they had not drunk, from bottles they had
not broken. But those gentlemen, in their nobility, could not
have outdone this lady, our genial hostess at the Alpine villa.

57

SCHULDIG

Let us say Nazis, not Germans,
just as we would not want

to be identified with certain
crimes our nation has committed.

There were innocent Germans,
just as there were Americans

who did not approve of Death Squads
a President called Freedom Fighters.

In 1945 a hundred and fifty thousand
were vaporized in a millisecond,

yet it is correct to speak only good
of that moment, as if cheering a game.

And what's proved? Men who scrawled
equations on blackboards later spoke

of their shame and fervent wish
they could unmake their bomb.

As for Germans, let us think of those
who looked at their hands, saw, smelled,

        and found no blood.

URSULA

Outside, affectionate eyes grateful for steak
and Rocquefort dressing, smiles and anecdotes
of prewar childhood Europe. We had held
hands in the dark theater.
                    She was terrified of everything
and the Psychiatric Institute was treating her
as a case history, the doctor seeing her every day.
It seemed she never ran out of terrible memories.

Some things are sacred, though I'll say this:
When she came out of that air raid shelter
fleeing the rapist, she was trapped in a ring
of fire, yet had to descend again, gasping
for air, facing him and the unseeing eyes
all around, as the next wave of bombers came.

A PHOTOGRAPH FROM 1935

For Kurt Klein

His parents sit at their kitchen table in Vienna
under a wall clock, its hands at five to twelve,
and when Kurt looks at the yellowed snapshot
he wishes he could go back and halt time itself,
since it galloped on to Auschwitz. He would leave
his father and mother there in their kitchen
with their hands on the table in their last days,
when they still thought of themselves as Germans.
He would leave his mother's hair up in a bun
and his father's mustache black, and he would know
the mustache had not been in honor of the dictator.

Kurt was a boy in knee pants when he saw the first bonfire,
books carried out and hurled into flames, gleeful faces aglow.
Later he saw the first Nazi motorcycle roar down the street,
and he still does not know how he survived to be
an old man in America. It took a number of miracles.
Had he not arrived at the factory just in time to disable
the bomb meant to blow up the young women inside?
Had he not been the first man to renew their faith
in humanity? And had he not found his bride there?
And yet it would not be kosher to claim miracles,
for it would not be fair to those who were given none.
He prefers just to say that even from boyhood
he always had a purpose in life.

SIGHTSEEING IN THE REICH

Near Buchenwald the Jugenstil houses
still stand with their wrought-iron gates
and their window grilles floral, their façades
of stucco depicting in bas-relief mädchen

whose expressions are unchanged,
were smiling and grimacing long before
Hitler's war. It's all a part of high culture,
the elaboration of beauty, the filigree.

The S.S. men who paused to admire
these faces trembled to be in the presence
of such elegance and looked dazed
when the name of the great Goethe

was mentioned or when Richard Wagner
came calling, even in the hands of
a pianist they murdered the next day.
After their homage to cold architecture

and to the kitsch in the local bierstübe
they went back to the living faces,
back to their work. That day of our visit
it was only woodsmoke, but you trembled

        and wept the entire night.

HOUSES

They were beautiful houses, the ones confiscated
by Nazi fiat. Charles Lindbergh was tempted
to accept a Berlin mansion offered, not long after

Kristallnacht, but that would have been another
public relations disaster so Anne talked
him out of it. Lion Feuchtwanger the novelist

lost his home because he wrote a satire unkind
to Hitler. By good fortune he was in the U.S.
when the Gestapo arrived. Compounding

his offense, he wrote a letter to the new owner,
addressing him as *Dear Occupant*, asking if
he was enjoying the hospitality, the amenities,

the library—although he should not be caught
reading novels where they were written.
He asked if the silver carpets had been stained

and if jackboots of the Brownshirts had broken
any tiles. He warned against pipes freezing
in winter and cautioned the occupant not

to risk losing this home, now his by virtue
of laws that transferred title although the Jewish
ex-owner was obliged to go on paying the mortgage.

Even an Aryan, the novelist pointed out,
had better be careful in this new age of terror.
And lastly Feuchtwanger asked about his pets,

the turtles and lizards left behind, and the flower
beds and the rock garden, and he wanted to know
if the servants had screamed when they were shot.

You can tell me all, he said, for writing
is my profession, knowing the truth and telling it
even when it is bitter and hard as hell to bear.

ONE THOUSAND YEARS

I always thought it odd that Hitler
planned for only one thousand years
and no more of Third Reich—
a modest request—not long
in the overall scheme of things—
not in the life of a star or a planet.
For only one thousand years
was it worth the expense of spirit,
the costly manufacture underground
and inside mountains of weaponry
distracting great minds from other
creative concerns? Was it worth
the firepower lost on London
or Warsaw, the planes exploded
in air, the arrangements for mating
of Aryan males with Aryan females
that they might produce babies
for Der Führer, human machines fit
to kill and be killed at the front
should the war go on for maybe
the entire thousand years?
Was it worth the sheer bother
of mass murder, convincing so many—
the thousands it took to undertake
on such a scale such a project?
Was it worth the effort, the strain
of thinking up lies, coordinating
schedules of planes, trains, menstrual
cycles and rockets, of keeping logs
in the books of the dead? Was it worth
losing the voice from raving in and out
of the stadium—like a lunatic, chewing

the carpets and tapestries? And did it
occur even once that he might not
be around to enjoy his Third Reich
for even a tenth of his thousand years?
Was a mere thousand years of earth
scorched and turned into necropoli
worth making an ass of himself?
And did he not know that the poet
Tu Fu had already opted for that
particular thousand years, well
in progress before Hitler was born
to a schizoid battered wife in Linz?

EICHMANN THE ETERNAL

> "The general impression seems to be that hanging was
> enough, and that the world is rid of him."
>   — Thomas Merton

He had prepared a few words
to be delivered at the foot of the gallows,
and as a speech they surpassed
even what his Führer had managed.
His lines could have been crafted,
of course, by the devil, who might
well have said the same thing—
that we were not through with him,
never would be, that we would see him
again and again—and he would not
forget those who had been kind to him—
as others in due time would be.
He favored certain nations, had blessings
for those like himself. Even as he spoke,
disciples were at work, the faith preached
with fervor, and thousands willing
to die in the cause of mass killing—
here, there, as children can tell us
in a recitation of continents,
nations, islands, current events.
What greater truth then than those words
Eichmann uttered before stepping up
for the noose as if mounting a train
for a journey from which
he would return. Again and again
we have already found him. Schoolboys
honor him and on the birthday
of Adolf Hitler become storm
troopers, S.S. men run amok.
"Your world is full of me, I am all

over the place," said little Eichmann,
"and whether you like it or not,
what I have done will be done."
He added that he was a believer
in God, *ein Gottesglaubiger.*
And why should he not, if
       assured of an eternal return?

BRONJA'S DELI

for Bronja Roslawowski & Tom McGrath

The hand-holding sweethearts looked like a pair of ebony
figurines out of Nigeria. He smiled, pointed to the glass
case, named their choices for lunch, but made no request
for advice. They'd get it for free. "You hear what I say,"
Bronja said, waggling her finger as she looked up at the boy's
face, "Love is better that way. And don't you get that girl
in no trouble. You keep peter in proper place. And keep it
clean, you hear? That girl, she deserve herself a proper good
mensch, not bad like maybe you. You play basketball,
that don't mean play around with no girl like my girl here."

The high school basketball star shook his head and smiled.
"Lady, you're just too much for us!" He regarded the green
number tattooed on her arm, the crossed European sevens.
"We never get used to how you come on." Bronja, squat
and buxom and bow-legged, waggled her finger again.
"You hear what I say," she repeated, then went back behind
the counter to make their sandwiches—the inch-thick
cheese and pastrami with black bread like those Tom and I
were munching as we watched. The couple did not
stay to eat what Bronja gave them, but were out the door
like a shot, the girl looking back with a smile. Bronja
may have been the only one in her life who cared, the way
she did for the neighborhood kids whose crayon art adorned
the walls. She waddled past our table as if running after
burglars, opened the door to call out her command
once more. "Don't forget, mein young mensch, you keep
peter in proper place." Tom and I washed down our last
bites of the sandwiches made with black bread. To hear
Bronja tell it, they had done her a favor letting her bake
such bread at Auschwitz, where she learned her good habits—

getting up at four a.m. A year or so after our visit
Bronja retired and sold the Deli for not much more
than a song to a ghetto girl, maybe the same whose virtue
she defended that windy day when Tom and I stopped by
for lunch and I suggested she write up her story for
the Yad Vashem in Jerusalem, telling how she had saved
her life by baking, shoemaking, and the art of rhetoric
                              in dealing with devils.

UPSTATE

There's an old Nazi who runs a motel
with an office that looks like a cabin
on a sailing ship. In the long night
his green neon flickers and junebugs
and gnats swirl around the bright globe
outside his door. If there's a hell
it might be right there in his mind,
or maybe he has no regrets.
No one else seems to care either.
In his captain's chair looking out
at the snow falling as if on the sea
he gives away none of his secrets
while down below the lovers rock on.

GEISTESKRANKHEIT

is illness from ghosts, brooding too much
on the past, letting those spirits, hangover

beings, take over, obsess you once again
with unwelcome facts—they *seem* facts,

and few are wise enough not to mind-read,
try with seeming help from those ghosts

to get it right once and for all. But speaking
in riddles, those devils confuse you the more,

mangle the mind. Who did what and to whom
will remain ambiguous throughout the centuries.

Be assured, your colloquy with ghosts, spirits,
is pointless. Only fictive crimes will be solved.

STRONGHEART, A MYTHICAL BEAST

"When you think of mankind, you can console yourself with
faith, hope, with Shakespeare, antibiotics, or with our footprints
on the moon. But with a dog, there can be no alibi."
— Romain Gary, *White Dog*

After World War II some Nazi attack dogs
were brought to the States, along with Hitler's
rocket scientists, cryptographers, and experts in torture.
Some of these handsome canines became seeing eye dogs.
But one, whose name was changed to Strongheart,
became a movie star. To say that he was a Nazi
is, of course, a matter of semantics, but he worked
under the command of an S.S. officer. Strongheart
did as he was told. He did not question orders.
He did execrable deeds we do not wish to contemplate.
Sometimes I am tempted to pardon him, and I wrestle
with such questions as innocence and rehabilitation.
Yet I am reluctant. Albert Camus wrote that there
are no executioners, only victims. Perhaps so. Hitler,
a child soon to be abused into evil, was as darling an infant
as they come, staring out at us, helpless as a doll
in his little white gown. But where can we go with
that thought? As for Strongheart, he committed
no crimes in America, though he sometimes looked
guilty. He was a handsome dog, a true Aryan,
a *wunderhund,* but in the war he had been a Nazi,
although he has defenders who deny it altogether.
Werner von Braun, who built rockets for Hitler
made the same journey as Strongheart, was presumed
to be an ex-Nazi. He was given awards for being
so noble as to improve his rockets and missiles for us.
They were no longer called "doodlebugs" as when
they took out a school full of boys near my wife's
childhood farm. In Strongheart's case we are dealing

with a movie star canine, successor to Rin Tin Tin.
He had fans, got sacks of mail every day, sniffed
with the suspicion he had been taught in Germany.
He ate filet mignon and wore a diamond necklace.
In films he attacked only bad men who had kidnapped
a child or robbed a bank. He lollopped across meadows
and over hills, intent to save lost children. He followed
his director's commands, though no longer in German.
At his master's feet—he slept with his trainer—
Strongheart was adorable. They say that once you looked
into Hitler's eyes, or he gazed into yours, you were forever
his slave. So it was with Strongheart, the death camp
attack dog I confuse with Rin Tin Tin and Lassie, the three
survivors who bark only to tell us of children needing rescue.

GRACE UNDER FIRE

> "Still falls the rain—
> Dark as the world of man, black as our loss—"
> — Edith Sitwell

They were such ladies and gentlemen—
those who were bombed—and after

the war the bombers were gentle as well.
"We're so sorry we *disturbed* Coventry,"

a German friend said to Osbert Sitwell,
who had nearly been blown to bits

in the Blitz. He had written to sister Edith
that it had been a "very tiresome night."

On another evening during the war
Edith was reading her poems in London

and was in the middle of "Still Falls
the Rain," which concerns the bombing.

It was as if the poem had become
the reality when those in the audience

looked up as they heard overhead
the drone of one of Hitler's doodlebugs,

the V-1 rocket that went silent when
its engine cut out—only then would it fall.

Dame Edith neither paused nor blinked,
but went on in her calm, unwavering voice

with the droning engine in counterpoint.
She must have inspired others, for all

kept their seats and were calm. And when
the engine cut out she turned the loud

pages and took her time picking the next poem.

THE WAY WITH DISSENT

Straight out of the nightclub
where he had told the joke.
Or arrested at home, no warning
in the middle of the night.

Take him, for what he believes.
Take him, for standing up
for humanity. Take him for
the wrong kind of patriotism,

throw him into the ditch.
Leave him there among birches,
their gentle, silvering leaves.
Put him in chains and a cell

for saying what had to be said.
Swoop down upon him if
he carries a sign with a message.
Indict him for trespassing on

his own property. Wipe his words
out of history, rewrite the history.
Yet some of us praise the rare bird
who sings with integrity,

the one who tries to awaken the town,
for we were born in the wrong land
to be war criminals,
                            some of us say.

WITNESSING

for Stephen Cary

Just after the war, he journeyed
to Auschwitz and Hiroshima
and Warsaw as witness for peace,

and later stood over a pit in Cambodia,
looked down upon bashed-in skulls.
He stooped and recovered the rubber

sole of a child's sandal, its straps
torn loose. He carries that talisman
wherever he goes, reminding people

how easy it is to let it happen again.
He passes around the sandal, inviting
us to think of the child who wore it,

fleeing for life until that strap broke.

HOLOCAUST UPDATE

Now that the Pope has apologized
for mistakes of his predecessor,
predisposed to love Nazis...

Now that Krupp and Ford and G.M.
have said they wish they had not
used slave labor, conspired

against even their own people...
Now that Xerox has expressed sorrow
for providing the machines

that sorted the dead from the living...
Now that Swiss bankers have shared
a few bars of gold with children

of survivors, who will never know
in what brick is buried the wedding
ring or the necklace or tooth filling...

Now that many of the faces are forgotten...
Now that not one cry can be heard...
you can give grief a rest, reaffirm

the best of all possible worlds, and debate
which of the world's cities is worthy of honor
as eternal center of murder and commerce.

AFTERTHOUGHT

"They always say 'merely surviving.'"
— Terrence DesPres

We who had no intentions of surviving
somehow managed, though that is always
a tentative matter. Yet it is not occasion
for pride. We can take no credit that random
Brownian motion, to which people as well
as electrons are subject, left us here and not there.
At certain times we might name, of course,
it helped to walk the other way, but we
were blessedly far from the killing fields,
and the victims were just by chance not us.

If we must boast, let us praise whatever powers
we choose that we mostly did nothing—
not driving, not drinking, not heading out
toward the stars as volunteers in spaceships.
And we left wars to others, for we were too
young, too old, or too frightened. Who died
in our place on the battlefield or in death
camps? Let us not ask, for we are pacifists,
merely surviving, and might not stand
a chance in a place of horrendous reality.

SINGER'S DECISION

Invited to dinner in Lisbon, Isaac Singer
took along a gift of two bronze roosters,
and from the moment he saw the hostess
she reminded him of his first love Esther,
whom he had never dared kiss—Esther,
who had been killed by the Nazis.

After dinner the host took out an ancient
book with wooden covers and parchment
pages, explaining that it had been hidden
throughout the Inquisition, when it could
have gotten many Jews killed had it been
discovered. Every page had been inscribed
by hand, in a painstaking, fastidious calligraphy.

But it was in Hebrew, not German, and had
survived earthquakes, flames, worms, rot,
and the hatred of six centuries of persecutors.
As Singer recalled of that night, the host
had kindled no light until the stars came out,
blazing fiercely as if just returned to life.

Singer decided that evening to return to America.
Begging his leave, he kissed the hand of the woman
who reminded him so much of his lost love Esther.

MILLENNIUM PRAYERS

At the stroke of midnight we said goodbye
to a thousand forms of murder,

hoped they would each and every one
go out of fashion. We would pray

for another style altogether, abolish
a few pastimes that do nothing but teach

murder and torture. But all we did was change
the name of the School of the Americas

where leaders of death squads are trained.
Yet we wished for the thousand years past

to be sealed like a tomb, and we hoped
the years ahead would not be littered

with corpses. Oh, vain prayers, not the first
men and women have uttered! Oh, grief

for the future that must be added to that
for the past! Oh, how we prayed for the brass

doors to be slammed on the abattoirs,
the horrors forgotten, the addiction to them

cured, the knowledge of how to inflict them
on others not passed along as heritage.

Lastly, we prayed that the sun would come up
on nothing it would be ashamed to shine upon.

PRIDE

There was much to tame in your life:
Therefore rejoice that you were not
Hitler come back to life—or even
your own father, who should have been
Field Marshall at least though his victims
were only pigs and his own mewling kids.
Nor are you the latest serial killer!
Despite a few mishaps with the gentler sex,
you were never quite Bluebeard.

But the bull still glowers and David
yet hopes to smite Goliath, at least once,
though there's no stone in his slingshot.
By now he should have attained
a peaceable kingdom or be enjoying
green pasturage like the cartoon bull
sniffing daisies, recalling how it was
to be adored in the stadium, cheered
though it was *his* tail and ears
the crowd had agreed to cut off.

Can pride be allowed for what you were not,
for not being part of a particular evil?
Can we give credit for thinning the plot?
There could, after all, have been more.
In the ring one bloody bull at a time
is dragged out in the dust, but elsewhere
the earth is allowed to tremble with loving.

LINES FOR SAINT SCHINDLER

for Stephen Spielberg

Oskar Schindler the playboy, *bon vivant,*
played cards for lives, knew how to act,

bluff, nudge an advantage. And if
the Church were not so ambivalent

about the Holocaust, he might well be
beatified, and in due time, canonized.

Of sainthood these days we can only say
it is earned with a command of political

skills not unlike those Oskar employed
on the fields of hell, so vivid you'd think

Bosch or Van Eyck had painted them.
Deniers can say the horrors

were only rigged photos. When Oskar
ran his remarkable factory of non-

production of weapons, blind to sabotage
by those who labored as slaves,

we could say he betrayed the capitalist
ethic, broke his contract, and yet

I say he outshone Kant and Hegel
as ethical philosopher. We leave

to another day the debate about whether
saints are allowed to tell lies to save lives.

THE WEEPING

"War is kind."
                        – Stephen Crane

At roughly the same time
the great men and a few women—
leaders of the world's greatest nations—

began weeping. The sparkling tears
ran down their cheeks.
And since this weeping

was televised like the Olympics,
millions joined in all over
the world, let their grief

cascade over their bodies.
They thought back on their wars—
visions of crematoria

heavy with ash, pyramids
of skulls in green jungles,
mass graves topped up

by the bulldozers—a hand or leg
here and there still discernible.
The desert sands were as thick

with the human as limestone
with crustaceans. And then
they asked us to join them,

these leaders, in their latest
attacks for good reasons—
the crusades they preach as essential.

And it was then, after fifty minutes
of weeping, that I decided
to join them. Indeed, I would follow

such sensitive men
even unto the death, through my tears.
And then they had the commercials.

THE GLORIOUS MILLENNIUM

It became something of a parlor game,
and the subject of every talk show—
naming the most important events
and advances in the last millennium.

A thousand years of progress—impressive!
A number of experts pondered the question,
praised our escape from the dark ages,
and savored again fruits of the Renaissance.

Doctors spoke of drugs discovered by chance
and the miracle of artificial hearts in the making.
Poets praised Shakespeare, and musicians
turned Mozart and Bach into nominees.

Italians got credit for Galileo, Leonardo,
and Marconi, but nobody mentioned Mussolini.
Germans could rightly be proud of Goethe
and Martin Luther, though it was too bad

he was such an anti-Semite—a bad influence,
admittedly, on the Reformation. The Bomb
was on everyone's list, though Einstein despaired
of humanity the moment he heard the bomb

had been dropped. Marvelous, someone said,
how one species had done so much, even cracking
wide open the secret of our genomes and D.N.A.
for now no more innocent people will be executed.

Looking back, there was not one scholar who saw
anything other than a straight line of progress.

I like to end my poems with ironic summations,
but in this case there's no way to top the one word—

Progress—affirmed with one voice by those
whose vision may have been impaired back
in the Twentieth Century by gazing too intently
through microscopes and telescopes.

VISITORS FROM AMERICA

We have now and then paid visits
to cemeteries with uniform headstones—
the military section of Forest Lawn
where my father is buried, the well-
kept lawn where my mother's third
husband—an army cook—lies waiting
as she wonders whether she will lie
on top or beside him. In France
I strolled a hill of white crosses.
In Vermont we took a morning walk
between stone walls, the kind Frost
recommended to keep neighbors
apart. Here headstones are treated
unequally. One man died in 1852,
yet someone has planted geraniums
just for him. Others who fought
for this side or that have earned
cute obelisks and one has an angel.

In a Ukrainian village a group
of Americans seek out what
was once the home of their family.
The current owner is genial, invites
the visitors in, seems glad to see
them. The wife serves drinks
and sweets. The children smile
at those their age. The hospitality
is flawless. And yet the nephew
of the uncle who was betrayed
to the Nazis risks being rude
by looking around, seeking
evidence. Had this been *their*

family furniture, *their* etchings
and paintings on the wall?
The visitor wonders if his grandfather
or uncle or the others glanced back,
said goodbye to the house and all
that was in it as they left at gunpoint
and soon stood by the open pit.
He asks his hosts how they acquired
their house. The *pater familias*
does not seem to know—he was
only a child at the time. He shrugs.
"After the war," he says, and perhaps
is glad his English is so inadequate.
He and his wife give frowny smiles.

"From whom did you buy?"
the visitor persists. But it seems
he is dealing with owners who have
no idea how their house was acquired.
They look around at one another.
The children giggle in embarrassment.
The host gives another frowny smile,
lifts his shoulders, his eyebrows.
How should he know—it's been sixty
years. But he offers a bag of apples
and his wife jumps up to get them.

Are these the apples of guilt, forgiveness,
evasion, sorrow, reparation? Are these
the apples that will undo the past?
Are these the blood-red descendants
of apples that grew in the yard that day
in 1942 when the family came out,
herded at gunpoint, nudged along
if they tried to look back? The visitors

take the path taken by those rounded up,
and despite sixty years have no trouble
finding the mass grave, though it is unmarked.
On a knoll near it they gaze at gravestones
of those who died of natural causes before
the S.S. arrived. A great aunt stares out
of a photograph framed in warped isinglass.
She still has the family face, but would not—
the children are told—have understood
English. The mass grave lures them back
off the knoll, almost glows out of the ground.
They stand looking down at the earth,
eating apples, aware they are not quite
                    the apples of paradise.

TALKING TO SHEEP IN NEW ZEALAND

A half hour's walk and we find them
up where the wind's a grand music
we seldom heard in the lowlands.
Their slant heads gaze down slopes
where gorse and the gold plumes
of the toi-toi hold them. Heads intent,
they hear and weigh what we say.
What wind from the valleys?
they ask—down where men decide
what to do—and not just with sheep.
Could rumor be true, fallen from clouds?
No wonder these humble sheep kneel.

And in the lowlands at Balclutha
on the South Island far from Europe
we breeze past a Freezing Works.
The concept is clear. The sheep
come in by train through the great
gate that someone opens on signal
and when it is very busy—thousands
processed each day—the gate is left
open for trains, boxcars one after another.
And then it begins. The sheep are not
told. Wool goes to one bin, tallow
of bodies to another. But sheep
have no gold in their teeth, no rings
on their fingers. It is Sunday and the docks
are clear and no smoke drifts from tall stacks.
Yet we speed up, thinking of friends.

SUBWAYS

for Adam Zagajewski

Their memories rarely collide,
though they carry them about
like little birds in cages.

They lug them into the subway,
let the cages sit on the seats
beside them. They look across

at others who carry horror
wrapped in newspapers, still
stinking like fish. The canaries

cheep through their shrouds,
for the gas did not take all
the life out of them. Oh,

little canaries, sing louder,
for the politicians are still
trying to murder us.

They are preparing the showers.

THE SHOES OF MAJDANEK

On the "witness of the witness tour"
students were shown the death camps

of Poland, and at Majdanek, inside
a barracks, a huge crib overflowed

with shoes of every kind, some
poking out through the slats.

Floorboards creaked as the group
advanced into the stench, gawking

at those rotting shoes, for there was little
ventilation or light. "All of a sudden,"

a young woman later said, "an urge took
hold, an almost irresistible impulse

to reach out and touch one of those shoes.
But then it moved, and I'll tell you, that

almost finished me off, scared me more
than anything in my life up until then."

When she turned around she noticed
on the empty bunks clothes folded

as if the dead might return and put them
back on. From that moment, she said,

she feared she might never feel gentle again
about anything on this planet called earth.

ON CAMPUS

I. YOM KIPPUR

It takes two days and nights
in hot Arizona sun for students

to take turns, standing in front
of the Student Union, reading

the names out over a microphone.
They do not know them all,

of course, but there are many,
a great many in each of the *Totenbuchen.*

The names are victims anew,
drowned out by lawnmowers,

leaf-blowers, roaring jets overhead
and motors of cars, trucks, bulldozers

and jackhammers remaking the world
in the image of God knows what,

maybe Hitler's architectural drawings,
until I, ever the gadfly, find a phone

and call Facilities Management
to demand some respect for the reading

of the names, but no one knows or will
admit who's in charge. Every God

damned one of them is only
                              following orders.

94

II. BAND PRACTICE

The girls diddle their red pompoms
with exquisite boredom

as silence reigns over the stadium.
The leader tells them to sit down.

The girls plop on the grass. Young
men lay down their gleaming tubas,

French horns, trumpets, trombones.
After a while the sun becomes

a problem. They're sweating,
burning—just as Buddha said.

Should they go on obeying
while sweat rains down

their faces? Are the titters
of amusement turning to fear

they will fry in the sun?
And will the orders coming

from on high become even more
absurd? Should they be a part

of this? Should they have signed
up for band in the first place?

God knows what the leader
will order next. Who will be

first to break away, march out
of the stadium? The horns

with great ears listen as red
pompoms and girls wilt.

And the answer's the same
as it was in the Nuremberg stadium—

not one walked away,
and the world went on burning,

        just as Buddha said.

III. HYSTERIA

I'd swear I heard Sieg Heil,
roars from the Reichstag,
wild cheers for Herr Hitler
offered the night sky—

oaths of obedience, eternal
fealty. They are eager
to follow him, wherever
he orders, and bring about

his thousand year Reich.
But tonight it's not Hitler,
only the coach, paid millions
of U.S. dollars, not wheel-

barrows of Deutschemarks.
He alone wins their allegiance
for life. For him and victory
they are eager to kill any enemy.

And I thank the stars
I cannot see for klieg lights
that it's only a football game
half a mile from our home,

and that none of these heroes
will fall at Stalingrad or El Alamein.

QUERY

How many years for forgiveness,
for the taint to be worn away
from each brick of the charnel house?
How many for the Kol Nidre to fade
into silence and the voices to disentangle
themselves from barbed wire and fire
and ash and history? How many thousand
years to write *Finis* tolling the last bell?

UNDER SENTENCE OF DEATH:
OCCUPIED FRANCE, 1943

This tribute to victims of the Nazi Occupation of France, including direct translation and transcreation of last words, is inspired by a 1954 study by Michel Borwicz entitled *Écrits Des Condamnés A Mort Sous L'Occupation Allemande (1939-1945)* (Presses Universitaires de France, Paris, 1954).

UNDER SENTENCE OF DEATH:
OCCUPIED FRANCE, 1943

i

What can we think of
under this sentence if

not of death? But to die
at twenty years was not

in the script—to be
no more than a corpse

like others thrown on
the heap with open eyes

still searching for God
knows what—a harbor,

a haven, or merely
the blue sky. Even that,

nothing more, would be
more than enough,

to embrace and take
into the years a sky,

allow it to darken
but only in time, each day

accepted with wide open eyes,
searching for God

knows what—a harbor,
a haven, a patch of blue sky,

not one's place on a heap of corpses.

ii

Listen, my friends, sing
any song you can!
Believe me, it puzzles them.
They won't know how to take it.

They never expected this,
singing right up till the end.
Believe me, it will impress them.
It will get under their skins.

La Marseillaise, that is a good one,
maybe the best. But any will do.
God save the King is a good choice,
also *l'Internationale*, excellent!

Myself, I have chosen *God
save the King*, just to practice
my English. God knows where
we will end up, calm and serene

with such music, even
the great Wagner and Beethoven.

iii

We live in a year well-designed to prove
the devil is all powerful. He controls

the night, can smudge it blacker than ever,
can block out the day with ash and smoke,

can extend to infinity the number of corpses.
And yet I have faith. Though we may not

see it, there will come a year that will prove
God is all powerful, could bring us back,

and might. I would like to think that even now
God is making his plans for a comeback,

that he has only been ill and is on the mend.
Soon this disease of a year will have run

its course. That is my faith, almost enough
to face what I must.

iv

We have a game
we play in the barracks.

Even there we manage
the game, and we smile.

We pretend we are back
at home. One of us

is chosen as the host.
The others are guests,

gazing around in wonder
and envy at all the good

luck, the quaint furniture
handed down through

generations. We inhale
deep the smoke of sweet

tobacco and the food
cooking. Someone says

it is a chicken. Another
insists it is wild pig.

We can almost taste it,
believe it is real.

We get to the point
of visualizing the wife

who is hostess,
another wife or two

as well. One is nursing,
with open blouse.

We almost believe it,
then someone

will say something.

V

It is customary to look around
as if you can see over the walls

and imagine what will remain—
the woods and the puddles

reflecting the sky, the roads
leading elsewhere, with ruts

of black mud, roads that reach
to everywhere we have come from

and everywhere we are going,
even to the day of revenge

called peace, when all the liars
find that no lie can save them,

when all the conspirators are held
to account though they speak

of their ignorance, their innocence—
how they could even be called

victims, how they did not want
to do what they will do this morning

and this afternoon and tonight
and tomorrow and the day after

for another year or a decade—
until the day of revenge called peace.

vi

The moon smiles stupidly in the sky
as if it shines down on a grotesque theatre

in which we are forced to be actors.
I and my friends are playing the condemned.

The Commandant is playing the Commandant.
The mice and lice and rats are being themselves.

There are playwrights, or someday there will be,
who insist on such scenes—phantasmagoric,

a huge moon bright as a klieg light
shining upon the piles of corpses,

but those will be bloodless as dolls.

vii

Do we risk hell
every time we pray

to that clay idol
we call bread?

The more desperate
the hunger, the more

tortured the dreams.

There is the theme of *adieux*,
first to the wife, then the infants,
and to father and mother if they are living.

Being so close to them now
you can call them back from their graves
if you wish, just to say *au revoir*.

ix

There is always this business of *Jamais Plus*,
never more! It has become an unfortunate tradition.
You could call it an addiction, an obsession,
or simply a mistake, and it is best not to begin,
even as one should never resume any other bad habit.
If you say one *Nevermore* you will be listing them
right to the end, mumbling, straying from the task.
Your list will be far too long, you can be sure.

Don't even start. When you say *Nevermore*
will the sun rise over our village in Poland,
you mean only that you will not see it.
You mean you will not notice the old man
at the window murmuring the Psalms.
You will not catch a glimpse of the Rabbi himself.
And you will *nevermore* see a Synagogue in Poland.

What you mean is that the Jewish children
like yours will *Jamais Plus* awaken, eager to tell
their dreams, which you hope will be empty
of this year and the last and no doubt the next.
When you say *Nevermore* for the thousandth time

you will be saying silly things and listing absurd,
unbelievably trivial things such as your lost toys
when you were that infant who will *nevermore* be
rocked in the cradle or awakened to tell dreams.
What you mean when you say *Nevermore* is that
you will *nevermore* talk with Yechoupetz or Zessez
and *nevermore* will you bump into Menachem Mendel
or Tovie Milchiker or Motke-Ganew. *Jamais Plus*
will you discuss these matters with others who desired
to write novels. As I say, do not get into this *Nevermore*
business, not for one moment, for believe me it is a lost cause.

x

Strange to have my moment,
to be singled out,

to end among walking
corpses and to be

a still one, as if
I were up to the honor,

old enough,
brave enough.

xi

Patrons of the arts—that seems to be the way
the S.S. officers, the more intellectual
among them—seem to regard themselves.

After all, they are taking good care of us
and often take the time to inquire
if we are managing to write any poems

or draw sketches in this atmosphere,
which they seem to think rather sordid.
With a whip the officer points out deficiencies—

as if we had not noticed. With a sigh he states
regrets for the necessity of such operations.
Aber der Dienst hat seine Vorshriften—Le service

impose ses règles—regrettablement. But how
could it be otherwise? We are all so helpless.
We know what the rules decree. *Neanmoins,*

we can make the best of things, and a few exceptions
can be made in support of the arts—*encourager
les beaux-arts.* Strict work details are flexible,

if authorized. A painter can be given supplies,
a composer allowed time at the piano in the officers'
lounge. He can spend a few hours acting

like Chopin—*comme Chopin.* A German copyist
is brought in to assure authenticity of manuscripts.
All of a sudden an S.S. man has produced an *étude*

or even a symphony, a poem or a philosophical
disquisition worthy of Camus, a man who writes
for *Combat* and is one of us. You would think

that Oberleutnant so inspired to quote Pascal
was himself a friend to the French and its culture,
to the survival of humanity. The great *Nous*

would include him for sure—the great *We*. Like it
or not, of necessity we have become collaborators,
calling upon our talent for survival. And as they pick

us off one by one our names disappear. We have been
ghost writers, phantom composers, disappeared
painters. And yet it has been an entertainment—

impressive, fascinating—to see one of these men,
the Commandant himself—discover a talent
so convincing that the next day he can brag

even to his poem's true author, whom he now names
and honors as his *influence*. "You inspired me...
You got the best out of me!" Effusive compliments,

cigarettes, relief from torture, can serve as royalties.
"Nous sommes collaborateurs artistiques," says he
of great talent in torture, after scrawling his signature

as if he were Beethoven. *"La musique,"*
he speculates, *"est le plus sublime des arts. Et l'art
rend les hommes nobles et la vie plus belle. Sans l'art,*

les hommes seraient changés en bêtes sauvages." Oui,
without art men would be changed into savage beasts—
wilde Tiere. It seems they could say our service—

this collaboration—was voluntary. An artist
survives for a while, though not long enough
to make a post-war claim on the work.

With golden egg in hand why feed a goose?
After the war, critics will note the French influences
and suggest that those who deserve credit

for all but torture and plagiarism were only running
an artists colony at Drancy, pursuing the Wagnerian
notion that all the arts could be combined into one.

And it is true that on days when screams provided polyphony
we assumed that someone was running the show,
conducting the orchestra, painting with blood, calling

upon every talent, be it captured, coerced, or seduced.

xii

Even the rags, even the gold
of our teeth,

even her hair, even my
broken wrist watch.

Everything is for sale here,
for nothing.

xiii

Others have made the choice
to abandon
this atrocious comedy.

Others like me
have decided to stay
until the last possible moment,

111

listening for bombers,
although I have not yet
heard even one

coming from the direction
we pray to, but
it passes the time.

xiv

Such shabby clothes
for a tailor,

much too busy
to make his own suit.

But they gave him no time.

xv

"One page," they say,
to the person of your choice.

But I do not wish
to serve propaganda—

for they would find a phrase
or extract a sentence to quote

in order to sort us out in their morale studies.
I wonder why they think

it makes any difference
what we think the night before execution.

But to manage good humor
the night before we mount the gallows

will at least bewilder them,
and if left in acrostics or riddles

an insult might survive the war
and our ashes.

xvi

At twenty years I am departing.
At twice that

I would still be reluctant.

xvii

We do not have much to share
or barter or sell to one another

but I offer a stanza of Shelley
and someone outbids me with Hölderlin.

Some nights the barracks
resound with Lord Byron.

"Roll on, Roll on, Thou dark blue ocean, roll!"
We can almost hear the English bard.

Old Victor Hugo makes an appearance
and the fellow who belts him out

says he is happy his professor
made all his students memorize

far more than anyone could foresee
any need for.

Strangely nobody knows any Shakespeare
except for a few odd scraps.

The man who could recite Lamartine
till the cows come home

went up the chimney on a quiet night
in December.

xviii

Near my house
there was a wood
and in that wood
there was a cuckoo.

Now, here in the care
of barbarians,
I hear that cuckoo
on the other side of my life.

xix

She was a foolish girl,
already sentenced to death,
a decision never reversed,
yet she wasted her last hour
asking fool questions.

How can you do this?
she demanded. *Yours
is the nation of Goethe,
Bach, and Spinoza.*

Not Spinoza!
yelled the Commandant,
red in the face.

Pearls before swine!
I muttered, but only
to myself,
looking away,
not brave enough
to shout those three words

out for her.

xx

The Commandant was a man
with well-shined boots
and a gleaming horsewhip
made of a bull's penis.

He spoke with precise, well-
chosen words, almost eloquent
if you did not consider
the context, at least until

he lost his temper, then ordered
the dog to lose his. It is an ugly thing
to see a dog becoming
such a man as his master.

xxi

My thoughts foresee each detail,
the last disobedient tears leaving my eyes.

I see as if in a clean mirror
the last grimace my face

can manage after I have left
off the effort to smile,

and I know what will be
the last word, but it will not

be uttered. Silence serves better
to catch the stone of one life

as it drops
into eternity.

xxii

Where are they going—
those who are ash
flying out of the chimney?

Where are they going, you ask,
and I tell you

they are going into history.
I tell you they are vagabonds

free to wander earth and sky,
and I tell you

I will join them tomorrow.

xxiii

They are proud to be assassins of babies,
throw them screaming into ditches, cover them up alive.

I will not repeat their obscenities,
attempts to turn murder into play.

They consider themselves masters of linguistic
invention and they hone obscene metaphors

like knives snarled against their victims.
But in truth this takes no great ability.

Anyone can renounce humanity
and descend to barbarism overnight.

For all their cleverness and brutality
not one moment stolen from the lives

of others can they add to their own.
The vanity and futility of their crimes

will follow them into the ditches of history
and their control cannot stretch even as far as the gate

out of this hell.

xxiv

For the first time in his life
he had a life worth the sacrifice

and we had given him the chance
to die in the bloody struggle.

He saw it that way
as he hurled the grenades

and saw how astonished they were.
But his prayers were in vain.

To fall in battle was one thing.
To be hanged at Drancy

at the hands of his countrymen
in thrall to the invader was another,

too much to bear. Therefore
they will list him—and me—as suicides.

xxv

One takes notice
that silence gathers around death,

that leaves fell, made a crown
for the partisan.

One takes notice
that friends, neighbors said nothing

though even the wind sang
and the animals looked mournful.

One recalls that a faithful horse
does not tremble,

that clocks strike not one strong gong
to tell the world of this.

One observes that nothing
bothers to honor this young woman

and all her murdered progeny
that will never be.

One takes notice
that God does not descend from heaven.

It is better to be far away.
But we take notice

at Varsovie, Drancy,
and Auschwitz.

xxvi

The moon smiles stupidly in the sky.
The stars demand of us where we are going.
All this evil we endure is a grotesque theatre.

Thus there are two kinds of gods—
one we imagine as compassionate,
just, and merciful—and another

we do not wish to imagine
though his orders are carried out here
with precision and servility.

Or perhaps there are just
two kinds of prayers
to the same intolerable god.

THE MUSICIAN

They called him a survivor,
one who emerged
from the terrible years

as an orphan. *What
will you do?* they asked him.
And at first he said nothing,

could think of nothing,
for grief had overcome him.
But then he declared

a purpose. He would try
to rehabilitate God.
He began with a violin.

Photo by Judy Ray

ABOUT THE AUTHOR

DAVID RAY's most recent book is *The Endless Search: A Memoir*. He has also received a National Endowment for the Arts fellowship for his fiction, as well as several P.E.N. Syndicated Fiction awards. He is author of fifteen volumes of poetry, including *X-Rays, Dragging The Main, Gathering Firewood, The Tramp's Cup, Sam's Book, The Maharani's New Wall, Wool Highways, Kangaroo Paws: Poems Written in Australia,* and *Demons In The Diner*. He was founding editor of *New Letters* magazine and *New Letters On The Air*. Other publications include *Fathers: A Collection of Poems*, co-edited with Judy Ray, and several other anthologies. He has traveled widely as visiting professor and to present poetry readings and workshops in the U.S. and abroad. He lives in Tucson, Arizona, with his wife Judy and their dog Levi.

Printed in the United States
1469000005BA/367-417